Fiona & Frieda's
Fairy-tale Adventures

Snow White and the Candy Apple

by Nadia Higgins   illustrated by Meredith Johnson

magic wagon

visit us at www.abdopublishing.com

Published by Magic Wagon, a division of the ABDO Group, 8000
West 78th Street, Edina, Minnesota 55439. Copyright © 2009 by
Abdo Consulting Group, Inc. International copyrights reserved
in all countries. All rights reserved. No part of this book may be
reproduced in any form without written permission from the
publisher.

Calico Chapter Books™ is a trademark and logo of Magic Wagon.

Printed in the United States.

Text by Nadia Higgins
Illustrations by Meredith Johnson
Edited by Patricia Stockland
Interior layout and design by Rebecca Daum
Cover design by Rebecca Daum

Library of Congress Cataloging-in-Publication Data
Higgins, Nadia.
  Snow White and the candy apple / by Nadia Higgins ;
illustrated by Meredith Johnson.
      p. cm. — (Fiona & Frieda's fairy-tale adventures)
  ISBN 978-1-60270-577-7
  [1. Fairy tales—Fiction. 2. Characters in literature—Fiction.]
I. Johnson, Meredith, ill. II. Title.
  PZ7.H5349558Sn 2009
  [Fic]—dc22

                                          2008038555

*For Cecilia, who insisted on this story when
my arms were too full to hold a book—N. H.*

Fiona

Frieda

Chapter 1

Once upon a time in a land not far away at all (in fact, just three blocks from Sprinkledust Elementary School), there lived two third graders, Fiona and Frieda. Well, at least on the outside they were third graders. In their imaginations, they were most often characters from fairy tales. For more than birthday candles, more than lip gloss, more than stickers, and even more than summer, Fiona and Frieda loved fairy tales.

Fiona and Frieda had invented a game called Fairy-tale Adventures. In this game, they would either act out famous fairy tales or invent new ones. Fiona usually cast herself in a role as Lady something-or-other.

"I'm the Lovely, Languishing Lady Olivia," she had said to Frieda just yesterday, holding out a gloved arm for a knight to kiss. Fiona liked names that rolled off the tongue. She especially liked the sound of *languishing,* though she didn't know what it meant. Then she looked it up in the dictionary and found out it meant "to be sick." So Fiona was the Lovely, Lively Lady Olivia after that.

Frieda wasn't really into princesses, but that didn't stop her from being best friends with Fiona. Frieda preferred a role that let her cackle-laugh or tip-toe creepily behind the sofa.

"I'm Frieda, the Languishing Lady of *Doom,*" Frieda had said to Fiona just this morning. *Languishing* suited her just fine.

On the fifty-seventh day of third grade, Fiona and Frieda had been playing Fairy-tale Adventures when they discovered something amazing.

"Aahhhhh-choooo!" Frieda had sneezed.

"Boo-hoo-hoo!" Fiona had pretend cried.

Accidentally, they'd said the "hoo" and the "choo" at the exact same time. Just then, fluffy white magic filled the air and everything went quiet. Then the only sounds they could hear were those of real fairy-tale characters. That's right. *Real* maidens like Cinderella and *real* bad guys like the Big Bad Wolf appeared right where they were—at school, the playground, even at home.

Fiona and Frieda realized they had magic rhyming powers after saving Cinderella and fixing the whole bowling slipper situation. As it turned out, the girls had a real knack for this type of work. They were fairy-tale superheroes!

Soon, Fiona and Frieda found themselves mixed-up in all kinds of real fairy-tale stories. Most of the time it was fun to be in a fairy tale. Sometimes it was hold-your-stomach funny. Once in a while it was so scary the girls were tempted to use their magic rhyming powers to leave the fairy tale for good. But they always had to find out what happened next. So far, no matter what, they'd stuck it out all the way until the "happily-ever-after" ending.

In addition to being best friends, Fiona and Frieda were also neighbors. The girls lived across the hall from each other on the eighth floor of Castle Apartments. Every day, they walked together to their school, Sprinkledust Elementary.

Fiona and Frieda liked school. But this Monday they absolutely could not wait one more minute to get there. Mr. Dennis, their new student teacher (and the greatest teacher ever) had picked them to be book buddies that week. That meant that at 10:15, they were going to walk, by themselves, to a kindergarten class. Each girl was to read aloud a book "of her own choosing" to the little kids.

"Of her own choosing." The words had echoed in the long, decorated corridors of Fiona's imagination. They rang out in the dark, enchanted hollows of Frieda's mind as well.

But Fiona and Frieda would not simply choose a book from the library. Of course, they would make one of their own. And that is exactly what they had done. Together, they had created a brilliant and beautiful rendition of Snow White and the Seven Dwarfs. The book was in Fiona's backpack this very minute.

"Let's take one more look at it before we get to school," Fiona said.

"Okay!" Frieda eagerly agreed.

The two friends plopped down in front of the eighth-floor elevators and opened the book across their laps.

Fiona and Frieda both loved to write, and they both loved to draw. At first, they had wondered who would be in charge of what. But, as usual, they had figured out a way to work together. Fiona got to write all the things Snow White said and draw all the pictures of the princess. Fiona also drew a flowering vine around the borders of every page. Frieda got to do the evil Queen's words and pictures. The girls had split the dwarfs, the prince, and the forest animals evenly.

Frieda admired Fiona's work with just a tinge of jealousy. "Your vine is beautiful," she said, "and I love how Snow White talks."

Fiona beamed. She *had* tried really hard to make the princess sound like a real fairy-tale character. For example, Fiona had been careful to make sure the princess always said "shall" instead of "will." Like when Snow White said to the dwarfs, "I shall never forget your kindness!"

Fiona had used such interesting words, too.

"Gallant . . . beguiling . . . breathless," Frieda practiced saying them out loud, even though she wasn't sure what they meant. And the words looked so perfect in Fiona's loopy, swoopy cursive.

"Truly magnificent," Frieda declared. That gave Fiona a warm, satisfied feeling. She knew her best friend wouldn't say so if she didn't mean it.

For Fiona's part, though she may not have admitted it, she was a bit jealous of Frieda's work as well. True, the parts Frieda had done were really creepy, not Fiona's taste at all. But they were so *imaginative*.

Take the Queen for example. The Queen had a different dress in each picture: one swirly and long, one with long sleeves like bat wings, one all pointy like a modern-art painting. Then, in the back of the book, Frieda had surprised her friend. She'd included something called an appendix. It included all kinds of extras that Fiona had never seen in a fairy-tale book from the library: a poem written by the mirror, a recipe for poison-apple soup, a timeline mapping out the story's highlights.

Fiona closed the book. "You rule, Frieda," she said.

"You mean, *we* rule!" Frieda corrected her friend.

Fiona giggled. "You're right. We rule!"

At that, Fiona wrapped up the book, and the girls headed off.

"This is going to be the best day of third grade ever!" Fiona exclaimed.

"Or at least the second-best one!" Frieda said.

Fiona had to agree. For no matter what, nothing could ever top the day the girls discovered their MRP. (That was the code they invented for "magic rhyming powers.") And those MRP would soon be more necessary than even Fiona and Frieda could have imagined.

Chapter 2

Ten o'clock. 10:05. 10:08. 10:09. Finally at 10:10, Mr. Dennis said, "Okay, Fiona and Frieda, you may go to Miss Crystal's class now."

Miss Crystal Clear was a new kindergarten teacher this year, and she must have been the best kindergarten teacher ever. First of all, she was really pretty, but in an interesting way. *Exquisite* was the word grown-ups used. Her laughing brown eyes were as warm as hot cocoa. Her skin was as smooth as the top of a freshly opened yogurt (before you stir in the fruit). She wore the most amazing lipstick, so her mouth was as red as the reddest crayon in the box. She also had the smoothest, blackest hair that she always wore tied in a ribbon. And every day, even when it was freezing outside, she wore a dress. And her dress always had a belt that perfectly matched the ribbon in her hair.

Most of all, even though everyone was always gushing over her, Miss Crystal didn't seem to notice. She was always too busy with her students. And her class seemed really happy. For one thing, they were always singing. Somehow, even though the kids did tons of art projects, her room was spotless and perfectly organized. "I don't know how she does it," the other kindergarten teachers would say when they walked by Miss Crystal's room.

When Fiona and Frieda arrived at Miss Crystal's class, there were only seven kids in the classroom.

"I guess a lot of kids are sick today," Fiona whispered, a little disappointed. She was hoping for a bigger audience.

When she saw her visitors, Miss Crystal stopped for a moment. She introduced Fiona and Frieda to the group. Then she said, "Ladies, would you mind ever so much waiting here for just a few moments while we finish up our

discussion of nocturnal predators? It's part of our endlessly fascinating unit on small forest animals."

"Not at all," Fiona said. She loved the way Miss Crystal talked. Meanwhile, Frieda admired the room. This unit must have been going on for some time. The whole room was decorated like a forest. The kids' artwork—squirrel sculptures made from bark, cotton-ball bunnies, a watercolor of a deer curled up in sunlight—hung from the ceiling and covered all the walls.

Fiona noticed how little everything was. "Look at those cute little chairs," she whispered to Frieda. "And the little desks and the little stools." Sounding as much like Miss Crystal as she could, she added, "Oh, and that darling little sink."

Bats . . . great horned owls . . . red foxes. These kids knew everything about nocturnal predators. Would Fiona and Frieda ever have their turn? Fiona squirmed. She twirled her hair around her finger, then she stopped. She wanted to look cheerful and interested in the presence of Miss Crystal.

Frieda did what she always did when she was bored. She made a list in her head. She listed made-up nicknames for the kids. That one with all the answers was Einstein, for sure. Then there was Sticky (with the glue stains on his shirt) and . . . she sniffed . . . Stinky. She snorted. This was too funny to keep from Fiona.

Frieda grabbed some paper and a marker from a nearby art station. She quickly drew caricatures of the kids and put their names underneath: Einstein, Sticky, Stinky, Crabby, Chatty, Smiley, and Handful. (He was the one who got orange cheese-curl dust on Miss Crystal's chair.)

"Pssssst," Frieda said, passing her drawing to Fiona.

Well, when Fiona opened the paper, there was no way she could continue looking cheerful and interested. Her whole body shook with laughter as she covered her face with the book. This made Frieda lose it, too.

Frieda waved to Miss Crystal. "Bathroom!" she gasped.

"Me too!" Fiona added.

Miss Crystal looked at the girls squirming in their seats. "By all means!" the teacher said.

Fiona carefully lay the book down on her chair. Then she rushed out of the room after Frieda.

Still laughing, she fell against the wall, slightly crushing one of the kids' artwork of a—was that a chipmunk made of noodles?

Another wave of giggles came over Fiona. Plus now she felt prickly and tickly all over.

Meanwhile, Frieda had gone totally silent. She had the open drawing in her hand and was looking thoughtfully at it.

"Fiona," she said slowly, "look at this again."

"Oh, no," Fiona said. "Please . . . stop." Her stomach was starting to hurt.

"No, I'm serious," Frieda said. She had that girl-detective face she always got when she was on the brink of saying something smart. "I believe we could have a fairy-tale emergency on our hands."

Chapter 3

It was as if someone had put all of Fiona's laughs in a box and snapped the lid shut. At the words "fairy-tale emergency," she went completely quiet and still. "For real?" she finally said.

"Let's consider the evidence," Frieda said in her Miss Sleuth voice. "Crystal Clear. Doesn't that name ring any bells for you?"

"Not really," Fiona said. "Crystal Clear, Crystal Clear," she repeated a couple more times. She loved the sounds.

"Okay, then think about her hair. Who else has hair that black and smooth? And why do you think she's such a forest-animal expert?" Frieda went on. "And furthermore . . ."

Now Fiona was thoughtfully silent. "Hmmmm," she said, starting to feel a little embarrassed. She wasn't usually so late to catch on to Frieda's theories. Obviously, Fiona had been too charmed by Miss Crystal to clearly see the situation. "The miraculously clean room," Fiona slowly said.

"And only seven kids in her class . . . ," Frieda picked up where Fiona had left off.

"Seven kids . . . seven dwarfs," Fiona continued.

"Crystal Clear is Snow White!" both girls shouted.

Fiona was on a roll now, and she started talking faster than an excited first grader. "And she's already hiding out with the dwarfs, which means the evil, jealous Queen is on her heels. The Queen could be getting the poison apple ready this very minute! How are we going to stop her? And what about the prince? Who is he? Where is he? How are we going to find him?"

Fiona and Frieda knew just what to do. They had to use their MRP and enter the magic realm of fairy tales that very instant. Luckily, they had made a long, numbered list of effective rhymes to use in just such an emergency.

"Number Twelve," Frieda called out. "On your mark, get set: Fairy-tale Adventure!"

"Happy tickle!" Fiona said.

"Snappy pickle!" Frieda said, at the exact same time.

"Hurry . . . hurry!" the girls muttered as magic swirled around them. They swatted at the white, sparkly stuff to clear the air. They listened for a second. The kids at the water fountain, Mr. Shinefloor's squeaky mop cart, the click-click of teachers' high heels against the floor—all the everyday noises of Sprinkledust Elementary School had gone quiet.

"It worked!" Frieda said.

Then, just to make sure, the girls poked their heads into Miss Crystal's room. *Clunk, clunk.* Loud and clear, they could hear the dwarfs noisily chiseling minerals for an upcoming science project.

Handful was having a time-out in the corner. "Can I come out now, Snow White? Snow White!" he cried.

"Shhhhh!" Snow White said. "Remember, until we're safe from the Queen, let's keep up my disguise. Dears, do try to remember to call me Miss Crystal."

The girls smiled at each other. Snow White, *the* Snow White, was a teacher in *their* school.

"Just as I suspected," Frieda said. And they were relieved, too. It looked like—so far—the Queen had not gotten to the princess.

But the girls had barely had a chance to even finish that thought when—

Haaaah-he-he-he-haaaaaa! Hoooo-haaaaa-heeeeeeeeee!

A witchy cackle rang out through the hallway.

"This is no time for acting, Frieda!" Fiona said, turning to give her friend the "shhhh" sign with a finger on her lips. But this time Frieda was not in character. She had her hand cupped over her mouth, and her face had gone almost as white as Snow White's.

Chapter 4

"**She's here**, the Queen!" Frieda hissed.

Haaaaa-ha-ha-heeeeee!

Another cackle echoed around the noiseless corridors.

"She's in the cafeteria," Fiona said. "C'mon, Frieda, let's go!"

Fiona leaned forward, her hands on her hips. She wasted no time going into action mode in situations like this. And it was a good thing, too, because Frieda looked more scared than a kindergartner on the first day of school.

"But, Fiona . . . ," Frieda found her voice. "What are we going to do? We can't just go beat up the evil Queen. We need a plan."

"There's no time, Frieda," Fiona said. Then she said the words Frieda always dreaded, "We'll just have to fly by the seat of our pants."

Frieda knew her friend was right. She numbly followed Fiona down the hall. Frantically, she tried to make a list in her head to calm down. But the only words her head would make were, "No, no, no, no, no . . ."

Fiona and Frieda stood at the cafeteria doors.

Hooooo-ho-ho-haaaaaaa!

"She's in the kitchen," Frieda whispered.

"She sure does cackle a lot!" Fiona whispered.

If Frieda sometimes acted like a world-class detective, then Fiona was just as cool as a daring and cunning spy.

"C'mon," Fiona said, using her in-charge voice. In spy mode, she slowly pushed the cafeteria door open with her foot. Then, pulling Frieda by the hand, she slid through and pulled them both flat against the wall. The two girls slinked toward the kitchen.

"Stay down!" Frieda hissed. The girls ducked behind the salad bar. They sat looking at each other for a minute. Something was off. They sniffed. It didn't smell right at all—and not in the usual way that it didn't smell right. It smelled like, well, the salad bar smelled *good*.

Fiona popped her head up to look. "Ooooooh," she said, eyeing the counter. "Today's ice-cream sundae day!"

Even Frieda couldn't resist taking a peek. Instead of cottage cheese and limp lettuce, there were bowls of ice-cream toppings. Crushed cookies, pink sprinkles, maraschino cherries, chocolate chips, syrupy strawberries, and more filled the counter.

But Frieda didn't even get a chance to say her own "ooooooh." For then, in the witchiest, creakiest, bone-chilling-est voice ever, the evil Queen spoke:

"Mirror, mirror, in my hand . . ."

"My *hand?*" Fiona echoed.

"Huh?" Frieda said.

They were way too curious not to check this out. They crept closer. They peeked through the serving window.

Fiona gasped. Frieda sucked in her breath. There was the evil Queen all right—as fabulous as she was terrifying. She looked like one of those actresses on a magazine cover at the supermarket checkout. She stood tall, taller even than Mrs. Goodshot, the school's gym teacher. And all that height was draped in a slithery,

snaky, gold dress that caught the light with her every move. Her hair, streaked purple and black, was slicked against her skull. Then it shot out in spikes, like a peacock's tail, at the back of her head. She had perfectly awful, long, witchy nails. Finally her face—

Each girl searched for just the right word.

"Creepy . . . ," Fiona said.

"Dazzling . . . ," Frieda murmured.

Her face was as royal as a lioness. Her eyes— the color of blue popsicles—glowed from their sockets. Her shiny, maroon lips curled up at the ends in a permanent sneer.

But what was most amazingly jaw-dropping was how the Queen looked so perfectly Queen-like—just as Frieda had always imagined her.

"It's like she's dressed up to play herself in a school play," Fiona said.

"Or stepped out of a page of a fairy tale," Frieda said.

Fiona and Frieda didn't see it right away. But, in truth, the Queen looked like she'd stepped right out of *their* book. The book they'd left on the chair of Miss Crystal's—Snow White's—classroom.

Chapter 5

"**Mirror, mirror** in my hand," the Queen repeated. She spoke to one of those mirrors that comes inside a makeup case. "Who's the most glamorous in the land?"

Now the mirror spoke. It sang out in a high, squeaky voice:

"Oh Queen,
The sight of you makes traffic stop,
but that Snow White—
well, she's tops!"

"Aaaaaaaaargh!" the Queen screamed. She smashed the mirror against the floor.

Then she went into a rage. *Slam! Crash! Bang!* Frantically, she rifled through the shelves of the cupboards, the fridge, and the freezer. She pulled out bottles of soy sauce, honey, vinegar, mustard, ketchup, and whipped cream. She grabbed jars of mayonnaise, marshmallow fluff, and honey. She gathered up cans of lima beans and peaches, boxes of mashed potato flakes, and wet bags of fish sticks and tater tots.

With this wild stack of goods, the Queen went to work. She tore. She smashed. She uncorked and uncapped. She sniffed some packages and threw them crashing against the walls. Others made her stop and laugh an evil "heh-heh-heh." These she gingerly shook and poured into a large soup pot on the stove.

"Oh vile goo,
Oh wicked mush,
simmer and stew,
ooze and gush . . ."

Fiona and Frieda felt like they were trapped in a nightmare. For they knew exactly what was happening, and it was all happening so fast. There on the shiny metal counter stood a ripe, red apple. The Queen was preparing the poison apple to knock out Snow White!

"A plan, a plan," Fiona whispered.

"Think, think," Frieda said to herself.

"What if we steal the apple?" Fiona thought out loud. But even as she said it, she realized the problem. The Queen could easily grab another one from the bins of apples in the cafeteria.

"Let's rush up to the Queen and throw the brew in her face!" But even as she thought out this next idea (and watched Frieda's lips start quivering) Fiona dropped it. She knew the fairy tale far too well to risk such a foolish move. The Queen's magic powers were known throughout the land. Even the huntsman had been too afraid to stand up to her.

"We could go and try to warn Snow White," Frieda offered.

"Also too risky," Fiona said.

Frieda realized her friend was right. By now, Snow White could be anywhere—the media center, the music room, the art room, the gym, the teacher's lounge. Would they find her in time?

"Plus, Snow White isn't exactly good at listening to warnings," Frieda added. After all, in the fairy tale, the princess lets the witch into the cottage, even after the dwarfs tell her not to let anyone in. So why would Snow White listen to a third grader?

Just then, a moldy, sour smell wafted over the best friends. Frieda gagged. Fiona covered her mouth. The Queen continued,

"Oh sour soup,
on you relies
my evil scheme.
Poison Snow White.
Dash her dreams . . ."

A plan. Think. A plan. Think. . . .

"Oh brew of ruin,
Oh stew of spoil . . ."

Fiona grabbed her friend. "Ruin!" she said.

Even Frieda broke into a grin. "Spoil!"

That was it! The girls would spoil the Queen's magic brew! But how?

Frieda stopped a minute to observe the scene. She scanned the floor, where all the ingredients the Queen had rejected were strewn and spilled. "Fiona, did you notice—," Frieda began.

Fiona followed her friend's eyes. She looked at the exploded can of whipped cream, the globs of marshmallow fluff, the dripping honey, and the spilled soda. "You're right, Frieda! The Queen doesn't want anything *sweet* in her brew!"

At that moment, both girls knew exactly what to do. They spun around. They scampered to the ice-cream sundae bar. Frieda scooped up a handful of crushed cookies. Fiona grabbed some pink sprinkles. They ran back to the service window. Then, they waited until the Queen turned her back.

"One, two, three—fling it!" Fiona said, and both girls flung as hard as they could.

Fiona's sprinkles pitter-pattered into the glop. Frieda's cookies plopped and sank. The brew gurgled and spit and even made a coughing sound.

"Who goes there?" the Queen said, spinning around. She prowled around the kitchen, looking behind doors and under counters. She even walked right up to the service window and looked out. But the girls were safely hidden, their heads completely covered by the counter.

The Queen peered into the brew. She sniffed it. By now, Fiona and Frieda's secret ingredients had completely dissolved into the magic potion. "Hmph," the Queen said. Then her long, jeweled fingers delicately grabbed the apple's stem and dipped it in. With a satisfied "hmmm," she held out the reddest, shiniest apple Fiona and Frieda had ever seen.

By now, Frieda was starting to relax. "It looks like a candy apple," she whispered to her friend.

"It kind of is!" Fiona replied, giggling.

Frieda laughed a little as she watched the Queen try to disguise herself as a lunch lady. The Queen may have had powerful magic powers, but she had no idea how to put on an apron.

"Crab apples!" she cursed as her head got stuck in one of the armholes. Finally, she figured out where all the holes went and she untied the string from around her neck.

The Queen must have been doing research on what normal people looked like, because then she covered her maroon lips with pink lipstick. She put on a pair of long feather earrings. Finally, she undid her peacock hairdo and brushed it with her long fingernails into a messy ponytail.

"Not bad," Frieda said.

"Actually, kind of funky," Fiona added.

The final result actually looked, well, cool and just weird enough to be sort of believable.

"Please work, please work," Frieda muttered, and Fiona knew just what her friend was talking about. For now more than ever, Fiona and Frieda's hopes rested on the altered potion.

Evil queens probably always keep spare mirrors on them, because then she pulled out another one and snapped it open. She looked at her reflection and turned her mouth into what the girls guessed was some sort of pleased expression.

"I'll show you, mirror, mirror," she said.

That must have been the Queen's idea of a joke. She broke into a squealy, hiccupy spasm, which the girls guessed was hysterical laughter.

Chapter 6

Next, the Queen swept out of the cafeteria, carrying the apple on a brown tray. Fiona and Frieda had no trouble following her now. The Queen was much too intent on poisoning Snow White to worry about a couple of kids running in the halls behind her.

Fiona and Frieda followed the Queen past the media center, past the art room, past Snow White's own empty classroom, and past the gym.

In the gym, Einstein, Sticky, Stinky, Crabby, Smiley, Chatty, and Handful were in the middle of what looked like a basketball game. Stinky sat on Sticky's shoulders. He held the ball just out of reach of the other dwarfs.

"No fair!" Handful cried.

"I hate this dumb game," Crabby muttered.

Fiona and Frieda quickly scanned the room. There was Mrs. Goodshot blowing noiselessly on a whistle. But no Snow White.

"She must be on her break," Fiona said.

"Of course!" Frieda said. "The Queen picked this time on purpose."

The details of the fairy tale were falling into place. Anyone who's ever read *Snow White* knows that the Queen waits for the dwarfs to be gone before she shows up with the poison apple.

The girls continued following the Queen
all the way to the teacher's lounge. The Queen
stood at the heavy, metal door for a second. She
wrinkled her forehead and curled her lips.

"What's she doing?" Fiona asked.

"I believe she's trying to smile," Frieda
replied.

Her "smile" in place, the Queen then pushed
open the door. The girls heard Snow White's
voice. "My, what a lovely, lovely piece of fruit!"
the princess exclaimed, as the door swung open.

Fiona and Frieda looked at the familiar sign
posted on the door: Teachers Only. The girls
peeked around the door's frame. They listened
as Snow White said, "For me? You're too kind."
They saw the princess reaching for the apple on
the tray.

Fiona glanced at Frieda. There was nothing to do now but watch—and trust that their plan would work.

Luckily, watching was one of Frieda's favorite pastimes. And sure enough, she soon spotted something really interesting.

"Fiona?" she said quietly, in that kind of question-voice that told Fiona her friend was about to say something really smart again. "Look at that orange chair next to Snow White. Do you see what I see?"

She sure did. "Our book!" Fiona said.

Even facedown, the book was instantly recognizable to its authors. "What's it doing here?" Fiona wondered aloud, though she already knew the answer.

"Snow White must have brought it," Frieda reasoned.

Fiona continued, "And why would she bring it unless—"

"She wanted to read it," Frieda said.

Fiona looked at her watch. "And Snow White's break is almost finished, which means . . ."

"Snow White has read our book!" Fiona and Frieda said together.

Just then, Fiona realized how much the queen in their book looked like the real Queen. "Snow White must recognize the Queen. She must know that if she tastes the poison apple, she'll fall into a deathlike sleep."

"What could she be up to?" Frieda wondered.

Both girls peered intently at the princess. She was holding the apple up admiringly.

"Why doesn't she throw it back in the Queen's face?" Fiona wondered.

"Why doesn't she throw water at the Queen and see if she melts?" Frieda added.

Just then Snow White dropped the apple. It rolled a little on the floor. The princess bent down to pick it up, and as she did—

Fiona jumped with delight. "Did you see that, Frieda? Snow White switched the apple with one from her pocket!"

Now holding the safe apple in her hand, Snow White took a hearty bite. She chomped on it in the most unprincess-like manner. She opened her mouth with food still in it.

"Delicious!" the girls heard her proclaim.

Fiona and Frieda were so mesmerized, they forgot they were supposed to be hiding. They stood in front of the door in full view, their mouths gaping.

Then Snow White was waving to them.

"Fiona! Frieda!" the princess said, welcoming them into the lounge. "Come on in. Girls, I'd like to introduce you to someone." She turned to the Queen. "I'm sorry, what was your name again?"

The Queen's fake smile had fallen away. "Miss Greenskin," she snarled.

"Miss Greenskin," Snow White continued, "these girls have authored the most imaginative story. You'd just adore it!" She winked at Fiona and Frieda.

"And, girls," Snow White was really hamming it up now, "you *must* try a bit of this amazing apple Miss Greenskin gave me. It's so good, it's almost *magical!*" she said.

Eager to play along, Fiona and Frieda each took a noisy bite. Then Frieda handed it back to the princess.

"Doesn't it make you feel just so . . . ," Snow White looked up at the ceiling, pretending to search for just the right word. "So, so . . . powerful and . . . and incredibly beautiful!"

"Give me that!" the Queen said, swiping at the apple.

But Snow White was faster. She quickly dropped the apple again.

"Oh, butterfingers!" she sang out cheerfully. "I'll get it!"

Then she bent down and switched apples again. This time she ended up with the poison apple in her hand and the one she'd bitten in her pocket.

"Here you go!" Quickly, Snow White shoved the poison apple into the Queen's hand.

Fiona and Frieda were following along perfectly. Snow White wanted the Queen to take a bite before she had a chance to notice that the new apple was different.

But Snow White needn't have worried. The Queen was so anxious to take a bite, she wasn't wasting any time looking at it.

Most of the Queen's pink lipstick had worn off by now. She opened her maroon lips. *Chomp!* She tore at the apple like a, well, like a nocturnal predator attacking its prey.

Everyone froze. What would the apple do? Tricked by Snow White, the Queen thought it would make her beautiful and powerful. Having read Fiona and Frieda's book, Snow White thought it would make the Queen fall over in a deep sleep. But only Fiona and Frieda knew the truth about the apple: Nobody had a clue about its magic powers.

Chapter 7

Needless to say, the Queen didn't fall over. In fact, she perked right up. She smiled a real smile with teeth and everything. Who knew? The evil Queen had a beautiful set of pearly whites.

Ha-ha-ha.

Then she giggled like, well, like a *nice* person.

Ha-ha.
Tee-hee.
Ho-ho!

Like a nice person being tickled with a feather—a pink feather. Maybe even a pink feather boa with glitter and sparkles.

The Queen was downright delightful. She clapped her hands a little. She hummed. She twirled around.

"Oh, I feel so, so happy! As happy as, as—," the Queen searched for the right word.

"Pink sprinkles?" Fiona offered.

"Cookie bits?" Frieda chimed in.

"Exactly! Oh you sweet, brilliant, little girls!" The Queen swooped down on Fiona and Frieda. She gathered them in a hug, picked them up, and twirled them around.

"Ring around the rosy," the Queen sang.

Frieda snorted, which made Fiona giggle.

"A pocketful of posies, ashes, ash—"

Then the Queen just froze. She dropped Fiona and Frieda on their feet. That turned out to be a good thing, too, because the girls were just about to lose it.

The Queen ran to the window. "Did you see that?" she asked. The Queen looked—could it be—concerned? Her eyes were even tearing up a little. "Poor, poor baby," she crooned. "I must help!"

And as the Queen ran out the door, Fiona spotted the matter of concern: Some little kid's scoop of ice cream had fallen off the cone.

"It is my duty to perform cheerful and kind acts!" they heard the Queen declare in the hallway.

And just like that, the Queen left Sprinkledust Elementary.

"Whooooo-hooooo!" Fiona jumped up and down. She high-fived Frieda.

"We did it!" Frieda shouted.

Then Frieda and Fiona did their own kind of ring-around-the-rosy dance, except the only words to their song were, "We won! We won! We really, really won!"

Who knows how long the girls would have gone on celebrating. But eventually they noticed that Snow White wasn't celebrating with them — at all. In fact, she was just standing in the corner with a worried look.

"Excuse me, Fiona and Frieda." Snow White shyly approached the girls. They stopped dancing to give the princess their attention.

"I can't thank you enough," the princess said. "That book you wrote saved my life. I'm so curious. How did you know about the Queen? How did you uncover her plans for the poison apple?"

Was she serious? Fiona and Frieda didn't know quite what to say.

"Everybody knows that," Fiona said.

"It's all part of your fairy tale," Frieda said.

"My what?" Snow White said.

"Your fairy tale," Fiona said. "You know, like *Cinderella* and *Little Red Riding Hood* and *Sleeping Beauty*."

"Kind of like your life story, at least up until you meet the prince," Fiona offered.

"You mean this story you wrote about me—it's all true?" Snow White said.

"Yes. Well, most of it, anyway," Fiona said.

"In that case, there really is a prince?" Snow White asked.

"Oh, absolutely!" Fiona said.

"But then, where is he? How will I meet him?" Snow White asked the same exact questions that were starting to run through Fiona's and Frieda's own minds. "In your book, the Queen's apple puts me in a deathlike sleep. Then I meet the prince when his kiss breaks the evil spell."

Snow White's worry was starting to look more like panic. "Do I really have to go into a coma to meet my prince?"

The girls just looked at each other. Each one could tell her best friend was blanking on a plan.

You know that expression, "saved by the bell"? Well, just then Fiona and Frieda were saved by someone yelling.

"Fiooooona! Where are you?" a voice called from the hallway.

"Did you hear that?" Fiona grabbed Frieda's arm.

"Frieeeeda! Yooo-hooooo!"

Frieda and Fiona smiled at each other. That voice. The girls would know it anywhere.

Chapter 8

"Mr. Dennis!" Fiona shouted her teacher's name as if it were the answer to a million-dollar question (which it kind of was, only it was even better).

"We can actually hear Mr. Dennis!" Frieda continued her friend's thought.

"Which means . . . ," Fiona started.

"He's a character in the fairy tale!" Frieda said.

"And there's only one left . . . ," Fiona said.

"Which means Mr. Dennis is—"

"The prince!" both girls shouted at once.

They dashed out the door of the teacher's lounge.

"Mr. Dennis! Mr. Dennis! Over here!" they called to their teacher.

Mr. Dennis ran over. "Fiona! Frieda! I've been looking for you everywhere! Where have you been? And what are you doing in the teacher's lounge? And what happened with your book? And—"

Just then Mr. Dennis noticed Snow White. He stopped and looked at her with his mouth hanging open—just like in the movies.

"Uh, hello, uh, I don't believe we've met," Mr. Dennis held out his hand to Snow White. Snow White turned into Tomato Red.

"I'm Snow White. I'm new here."

"I'm Dennis. I'm new, too."

"It is my deepest pleasure to meet you," Snow White said in her lovely, princess voice.

"No, the pleasure is all mine." Mr. Dennis actually bowed at the waist like the real prince he was.

Frieda nudged Fiona, and Fiona nodded. This was the time in the fairy tale when the grown-ups needed to be left alone. And besides, the girls still hadn't had the chance to read their book aloud. Fiona grabbed the book from the orange chair. "Ready?" she said to her friend.

"Ready," Frieda said.

"Three, two, one . . . candy apple," Fiona said.

"Rusty cackle," Frieda said.

After a few seconds of magic dust, they were back outside Snow White's classroom. "Hey," they heard Smiley say, "when are we going to get to hear those big girls read their book?"

The girls smiled at each other. They'd created an amazing, beautiful book. They'd turned the poison apple into a magic candy apple. They'd helped trick the Queen in the teacher's lounge. They'd led the prince to Snow White.

And now, at last, they were finally going to have the chance to be book buddies. Frieda gave Fiona a nudge and said, "You know, maybe this day could tie as the best day of third grade ever."

"It's at least as good as a candy apple!" Fiona joked, and the two laughed all the way into Snow White's tidy classroom.

It turned out Mr. Dennis and Snow White did have a lot in common. They both loved kids, obviously. And when Snow White found out that Mr. Dennis volunteered once a week at a wild animal rescue shelter, she could have kissed him.

Snow White's little house on Cottage Drive was on Mr. Dennis's way home. In fact, his place at Happy Endings Townhomes was just another block down the street. So he offered to give her a ride home the day they met. The next day she drove him. Pretty soon they were carpooling. After a couple of weeks, Mr. Dennis got up the guts to invite Snow White over for dinner.

Many months later, Snow White, inspired by Fiona and Frieda's book, wrote her own, real-life story. The story became a best seller, and Fiona and Frieda practically memorized it.

On page 162, Snow White wrote about the night at Happy Endings Townhomes when she and Mr. Dennis had their first kiss. She wrote that, at that instant, she knew in her heart that she wanted to marry him. And she wasn't asleep at all. In fact, as she put it, her heart was beating "faster than a wild rabbit's."

Not too long after that, Mr. Dennis and Snow White got married at a huge party at the Sprinkledust Elementary gym. The theme for the party was "Enchanted Forest," and Snow White's class made all the decorations—including a life-sized mural of Snow White and Mr. Dennis riding toward a castle on a white horse (inspired by Fiona and Frieda's book, no doubt). Fiona and Frieda made the programs, at Snow White's special request. Even the Queen showed up to make balloon animals for all the kids.

And that's the story of how Snow White tricked the Queen, met her prince, became a famous author, and lived happily ever after.

The End

#13. Candy apple . . .

rusty cackle . . .

#12. Happy tickle . . .

snappy pickle . . .

#11. Macaroni art,

lunchroom cart!